CONSTANCE ANN IN HOLLYWOOD

Written & Illustrated

By edwin gilven ©

All Rights Reserved

ISBN: 978-0-359-45592-8

Foreword

To all the young dreamers and the crime fighters from within! ~ Meet Constance Ann, age 6. Her best friend Mary Margaret, age 6 and a half and our tumbling genius Elliot, age 7.

In truth, they were all exceptional geniuses living in Johnsville, Vermont solving mysteries and problems in the lives of the young children and sometime even the lives of the old ~ *The Adventures of Hollywood'*

Shall we meet them inside ~

Acknowledgement

I would like to take this time to thank my brother Ron Gilven and his family, my sister Phyllis Gilven Enzor, Richard Jones and family, my sister-in-law Simone Tate & family, Sister Filmore & family, Connie Abernately (Constance Ann), Larry Marks, Ken & Tina Krick and staff. Michelle Bentz and family, My boyz at Last Stop Computer, Goodfellas Barbershop, Tami Elliott (My Citizen), Teri Lowe Dodge, Stan Smith, Sharon Lacey (Comedian), DeanneMichelle', Stan (the man) Skinner, Marco Cabañas, Douglas Wood (Kingfish), Brandi Westerhausen, Mr. Hunter & wife Virginia owners of Tuff T's, My neighbors on East 64th Street, 98404. The families of; Willee Shenkel, Kenny & Michael Bush, Curtis Dahlgren, Jim Riley (Bodeen), Ralph Tipton, Tyler Johnson, Gary Pisani, Ron & Teresa Kelly, Varriece Spice, Eddie Gales. Thomas Barr.

My friends from a far; Floyd Hall, Sr. & family, Nathanial (Lamont) Thompson, and Mr. John Robinson and his wife, Janice; I must also thank my Higher Power, and *so many others for their supportive love and rich encouragement.* Their never-ending belief in my work has been a great inspiration. For without their daily persistence this book would have not been possible ~ much love and respect to you all! And **sooooooo many more!**

A Special Dedication to my parents, Mr. & Mrs. Gilven, who are now long gone from this world, Love you, both! -

Again, I thank you all!

edwin

CONSTANCE ANN
IN HOLLYWOOD

Still on summer vacation the young detectives from Vermont and their parents are on the last leg of their long trip ~ Hollywood!

"Here's looking at ya, kid!" giggled, Elliot as he pinched Mary Margaret's cheeks! She protested!

"Elliot, stop it! You're no movie star! And Humphrey Bogart you're not!" Elliot smiled then ~

"*Et-et-et-et*-et!" it was Constance Ann! She wore an over sized army helmet and carried a huge toy machine gun! She continued, "*Et-et-et-et*-et!" Ha, aha, ha! Boy, this acting stuff is fun! Elliot, you think your father's friend will let us play all day in this studio? I like this! *Et-et-et-et*-et!" Elliot, laughed as she pretended to shoot him,

"Of course, they trust us! Besides, Mr. Welsh is my father's oldest college friend or something ~ also Dad already told me we could stay all day on the set of 'Battle Zone!'"

"Oooow, Connie, who's the Stars?" shouted, Mary Margaret! Constance Ann tugged on Mary Margaret's arm with enthusiasm herself, "Mel Gibson?! Tom Cruise?! Who?"

"I don't know," answered Elliot. He continued, "Dad said that they aren't shooting any scenes today. But Mr. Welsh's son Andy will give us the grand tour." Elliot looked about the huge studio hanger, then,

"Hey, Elliot!" It was Andy! He was the same age as Elliot (7 yrs old). He bristly trotted over to them. He hugged Elliot and happily rubbed Elliot's hair! He shouted, "Dude! Aha, ahaha! Father told me you were here, wow!" Andy turned toward Constance Ann and Mary Margaret, and asked ~ "Who are your friends? Hi, my name is Andy, and yours?"

"Constance Ann."

"Lady Mary Margaret." Constance Ann nudged her best friend in her side with clinched teeth as she whispered to her, ~ Mary Margaret-t-t-t, that's Mr. Welsh's son . . ." But,

"Lady Mary Margaret, please to meet you!" Andy pulled 2 fake flowers from one of his pants pockets and gave one to both girls. Elliot covered his face with one of his hands as he tried to hide his face. He playfully snickered at them. He spoke,

"Ahh-h, Lady Mary Margaret, aye, such a marvelous lass, she be-e-e!" Elliot laughed aloud as he reached into his pockets and gave both girls a piece of bubble gum!

"Hey, where's mine," questioned, Andy!

"I'm all out, Andy, sorry."

"Here," interrupted, Mary Margaret, "take mines." She handed her bubble gum stick to Andy. Andy turned to Constance Ann and asked,

"Well?"

"Well, what?" replied, Constance Ann.

"Aren't you going to give me yours, too?" answered, Andy. Constance Ann stared at him as she placed her bubble gum stick into her mouth; she spoke, "No-o-o, why would I want to give you mines. Mary Margaret gave you hers? Don't be greedy now, Andy!"

"I'm not greedy," shouted Andy! "And you can call me, Andrew!"

"Fine with me," calmly answered, Constance Ann.

"Hey, hey . . . guys!" It's only gum," cried, Mary Margaret, then Elliot spoke, "Gee, Andy, Constance Ann is cool. Come on let's play some games!

"Yeah!" cried, Mary Margaret! "Andy, can we dress up in different costumes?" Andy smiled; then answered,

"You, bet we can! Come on!"

They followed their host outside Studio 18 to Studio 13 and there they each found the costume of their liking ~ Andy wore a huge hat that had the words MAD HATTER written on it! Mary Margaret wore a lady gladiator outfit ~ Constance Ann's costume was that of a clown with bushy orange and blue hair ~ and Elliot was . . .

"Robin Hood, I'm Robin Hood!" Elliot slowly twirled around to show off his green outfit. Mary Margaret asked,

"Are those arrows real?" she pointed to his arrow quiver.* *(*arrow quiver is a leather container for holding arrows)*

"Yeop, they're real, but not that sharp ~ here, feel one!" He let Mary Margaret feel one. Then, she gave the arrow to Constance Ann ~ "Here, Connie."

"Whoa-a, cool," cried, Constance Ann, she continue, "Andrew, did you know that Elliot really is a good marksman with the bow and arrow! Really, he is!" Andy looked at Elliot with a surprised smile. Mary Margaret spoke ~ "He sure is! He won the 2nd grade bow and arrow contest last year! Huh, Elliot?" Elliot blushed; and, shyly answered,

"Ah-h, well, kinda."

"Kinda!" shouted, Constance Ann! "Show him, Elliot! Come on!"

"Naw, come on, let's play. What will we play?" Andy eyes opened wide with excitement, he spoke,

"Hide and seek! This is a big lot with many different stage props! It'll be fun trying to find each other. I've already pre-programmed them to come on when any of us enters into them." Andy ran over to a box of toy guns! He shouted, "Look, paint pistols! They shoot color paint

8

balls!

"Don't those things hurt?" questioned, Constance Ann.

"Nope, these paint balls are made out of sponge, just kinda messy ~ see." *PTZZT!* He shot Mary Margaret's left ankle! *SPAT!*

"Hey-y!"

"Ha, ha . . . see, didn't hurt. Did it? Ha, ha, ha!" Mary Margaret giggled at herself ~ "No-oo, it sure didn't! Let me see one of those pistols!" Constance Ann looked at her best friend ankle ~ she giggled as she pointed to the ankle,

"Ha, ha, that looks so funny! Mixed match shoes!"

"Funny, fun-ny, ha, ha, I should splatter you!" Mary Margaret was smiling herself ~ then

"Well, is it a go?" asked, Andy! They all agreed and Constance Ann was IT! She would have to find her friends ~ of course, she cried foul play, she complained,

"That's not fair! We're your guest ~ you should be IT, Andrew!"

"But, I'm not, it's you!"

"Come on, Connie, be a good sport about it!" replied, Mary Margaret ~ Constance Ann protested once again,

"But, that's not right and he knows I'm right . . . . soooo!" *PTZZZT! SPAT!* Constance Ann shot Andy's big hat off of his head and ran off laughing as everyone quickly shot their paint balls at her as she ran away giggling! For in truth, it was going to be a fun time in Studio 13!

MUCH LATER:

As Constance Ann quietly crept throughout set 18, she entered stage 4 filled with tall cartoons *backdrops ~ *(*painted scenery on either canvas or wood)* *SPAT! SPAT!* Wet sponge paint balls splattered just above her head! She giggled as she ducked for shelter behind a picture of a bear! She slowly poked her head out ~ *SPLAT!* A sponge paint ball just missed! She ducked back down and giggled! She shouted, "*Olly olly oxen free!" She heard

Elliot voice echoed with laughter, *(*roughly translated to "Come out come out wherever you are.")*

"Ha, ha, yeah, right!" Then she heard Mary Margaret's voice ~ "Girlfriend-d-d, we see you-u-uu! Come and find us! Ha, ha, ha!"

"Over here-e-e!" it was Andy! Then Constance Ann heard footsteps running off! She cautiously stepped from behind the painted bear and chased after the footsteps!

Several minutes, later on the set of a ruined city ~

"Hah, gotta, Elliot!" *SPLAT!*

"Aargh!" grumbled, Elliot! He turned toward his friend with a disappointed smile and sorrowfully spoke,

"You're good. I was hid pretty well." Then he laughed with that patent smile of his ~

"Yep, I am pretty good, buddy!" answered, Constance Ann. She smiled and continued, "Now, you're on my team! We'll definitely find Mary Margaret and Andrew!" Constance Ann with her clown outfit on twirled the toy gun around on her fingers and pretended to blow smoke from the barrel. Elliot spoke,

"The last time I saw Andy, he was over in the futurist prop!"

"Where's that?"

"I think it's on stage 7!" Suddenly without any

warning the lights went off! *BLINK!* Then the emergency lights came on! The whole building was lit by dim yellow lights! Next, they heard!

"Connie! Help! Connie! Conn' . . ." then they heard no more!

"Elliot . . . Elliot?" whispered, Constance Ann! He whispered back,

"Yeah?"

"That was Mary Margaret! She's in trouble." Constance Ann cupped her hands around her mouth and shouted, "Mary Margaret-t-t-t! Mary Margaret-t-t!" They waited; no answer! When suddenly!

"Detective, watch out!!!" One of the large wooden prop slowly began to fall toward Constance Ann! Elliot pushed her to safety and away from disaster! *BAM!!!* Yellow dust particles immediately floated up from the hard floor. Constance Ann on her stomach, cried out, *"EECK!"* she had accidently smashed her toy paint pistol. Paint stained her costume. "Look!" she shouted, "The paint glows, wow!" Elliot looked at his shoulder where he was tagged by Constance Ann. It radiated a large patch of lime green! He spoke,

"Mmm-m, we definitely can be seen now!"

"Yeah, we sure can! I betcha Andrew is behind this!"

"Come on, Detective, just because you two had an argument doesn't mean he is behind this ~ he's probably just as confused as we are." Elliot helped Constance Ann to her feet. She looked at Elliot paint gun ~ "Your gun is broken too? She pointed at it. Elliot smiled as he pulled one of his arrows from his quiver. He spoke with a soft smile ~ "Look!"

"Whoa-a-ah, that's cool, Elliot!" excitedly responded, Constance Ann! "You put your paint balls on the tips of your arrows!" Elliot teasingly raised his eyebrows and spoke ~ "I thought this would be much funnier! Then!

"Elliot!" it was Andy! His mad hatter hat was torn on one side. He ran up to them. He was totally exhausted as he spoke fast and nervously loud! "Ah, boy! *(puff)* I barely got away! *(puff)* Teenagers! They broke into the studio; they are vandalizing everything in sight!" Constance Ann grabbed the exhausted Andy

"Where's Mary Margaret!?"

"I left her!" replied, Andy! Elliot grabbed Andy by his shoulder and quickly turned him around, he shouted, "You left her! You left our friend alone with teenagers?!"

"I-I-I had to! They chased me away!"

"Where did they take her?" asked, Constance Ann! Andy pointed behind Elliot's shoulders,

13

"There! We must go that way!" Andy lead the way in the yellow lighted studio ~ next, he wandered over to an electrical box and ~

"There ~ we have light, now!" shouted, Andy. The two children from Vermont discovered that they now stood in the middle of another set ~ The North Pole! It was a huge set about the size of a football field and it was

"Cold!" shouted, Elliot!

"Of course, it's cold! This is the Antarctic Set!" answered, Andy ~ frost came from their mouths. Constance Ann asked with a doubtful stare, "We don't have to cross that snow do we. I'm not dressed for it." Then a faint sound was heard in the cold air, it was Mary Margaret. She pleaded for help! You could barely hear her cries for help ~

"Sh-h-h, quiet, listen!"

"Connie-e-e! Please help me! Connie-e-e-e!"

"That's Mary Margaret's voice!" shouted, Constance Ann as she grabbed Andy by his torn clothes. She angrily yelled at him! "You coward, you left my best friend!"

"Detective," shouted, Elliot! But, Constance Ann kept yelling at Andy! Elliot grabbed his best friend by one of her arms! She knocked his hand free! Andy pushed Constance Ann! She stumbled back! Elliot stepped

between the two ~

"Andy, listen, Constance Ann is my friend, please don't push her ~ don't you understand? Our best friend needs our help! We need your help, not your anger!" Andy smiled and spoke,

"Well, tell Ms. Pickle face to back off! I told you guys, I had no choice . . . I'm sorry. I am sorry!" Then he began to cry uncontrollable. But, Constance Ann wasn't moved by his tears. She just walked pass him onto the snow. Elliot followed her and Andy followed him.

About halfway into the journey it began to snow hard. The wind started to howl! Constance Ann noticed Elliot had stumbled due to the coldness! She stopped and went back to help him up, she spoke,

"Kinda cold, eh, come on, Elliot, we're almost out of this snow." Then suddenly the frozen ice from under them began to crack and break up!

"Run!" screamed, Andy!

"Help, me, Andrew! Help me with Elliot!" But, Andy didn't; he ran as fast as he could away from them! Constance Ann quickly pulled off Elliot's bow and grabbed one of his arrows with the paint ball tip! She yelled!

"Coward!" And then she carefully aimed the arrow at Andy as he scrambled and ran in the snow and confusion! *ZIPP-P-P-P!! SPLAT!*

"Gotcha!" Little Andy was hit square in the back! A florescent lime yellow colored his back! He fell onto his face! The wind howled even louder then, the ice erupted! The large field was no longer solid! The ice was breaking up! Huge chunks of ice dipped and floated about! *SPLASH!* Andy slid into the water! Constance Ann screamed to Elliot as they tried to balance themselves on the ice!

"Elliot, I can't hold on! We are going to . . ." *SPLASH! SPLASH!* Their little heads disappeared beneath the trouble water! Then Elliot's head shot up and out of the water! Constance Ann was next! Elliot gasped for air! He reached for Constance Ann ~ "Hey, this water is warm! It's like a big swimming pool!" Constance Ann with her fake clown hair drooping to one side smiled back at Elliot and agreed ~ "Hey-y, this is cool!" She swam toward him and pointed ~ "There's goes your buddy." She had pointed at Andy who had reached dry snow and scurried into another section of the studio! Elliot and Constance Ann struggled through the howling wind and snow until finally, they stood on dry snow! Elliot, blew some air from his mouth with relief, "Whew-w-w, wow, what an afternoon!"

"I know, and . . ."

"Conni-e-e-e! Help me! Con-nie-e-e!" Elliot looked at Constance Ann and saw that she was visibly worried, he spoke,

"Don't worry, Detective, be concern, but don't worry, worrying does little good for any of us." Constance Ann slowly pulled her clown wig off and softly dropped it on the dry snow. She spoke softly, "Come on, and lets find our friend."

Several minutes later, they were on a different set ~ The Desert!

"Oh, wow! From cold to heat!" cried, Elliot! He continued, "Another football field. Well, at least it'll dry our clothes. Then he noticed, "Hey, your paint is gone!" He pointed to the front of Constance Ann's costume! "I guess that water washed it off!" Constance Ann still silent looked down at her outfit and continued to walk on emotionless.

LATER:

About 30 yards from the next set the two detectives sat down to rest. Elliot spoke,

"Ah-h-h-h, rest, boy it is hot, isn't it? Amazing how this place seems so real!"

"Yeah, it does, answered, Constance Ann.

"Detective? What do you make of all of . . ." Elliot's eyes froze and widen. He slowly reached for his bow and arrow. Constance Ann slowly looked up,

"Huh? What were you asking me?" Then her eyes froze and widen. She yelled! "Elliot, why are you pointing that paint arrow at me?" Then she heard the sound of a rattle! It rattled again and again! It was a rattlesnake and it was about to strike! Elliot with beads of sweat on his forehead carefully moved his head to shake the moisture free. He spoke softly,

"Don't move, Detective . . . it might be real. Please do not . . . move." Little Constance Ann did all she could not to scream or move. She trembled with fear;

then, the snake attacked! But, so did Elliot! *SPLATT!* Bullseye! He hit the snake right on his forehead and knocked him backward with his paint ball. The now blue color rattlesnake slithered off behind some rocks! Constance Ann placed her hands on her chest and sighed with relief! Elliot smiled and raised his eyebrows teasingly at her! But, it was no time for glory, because suddenly the sky was filled with a strange sound! *WHEEEEEEEEEEEEEEEEE-E-E-E-E-E!*

"In coming, bomb!" screamed Elliot! He grabbed Constance Ann and pulled her away from the rock! He yelled! "Hit the ground!" *BOOM!!* Fake pieces of rock and dirt filled the air! *WHEEEEEEEEEEEEEEEEEEEE!*

"Run!" *BOOM!! WHEEEEEEEEEEEE! BOOM!!!*

19

"Elliot!" screamed, Constance Ann, "We're being bombarded by those teenagers, I bet!!! *BOOM! WHEEEEEEEEEEEEEEEEEEEEEE!*

"Run for that prop," Elliot pointed! Run!!! *BOOM!!* As they ran toward the new stage prop, the bombing suddenly stopped, only to be replaced with ~ *BLAM!!! BLAM!!!* They dove into the new set! The Battle Zone!

"Stay down," cried, Elliot! *BLAM!!!*

"Elliot, look!" screamed, Constance Ann! It was a tank! Constance Ann had stood up to point at the tank! Elliot yelled as he ran toward her ~ he dove, the tanks fired a round! *BAM!* Elliot knocked his friend to safety! The shell hit an old building and debris flew everywhere! *Ratt-tat-tat-tat! Ratt-tat-tat-tah!* It was machine gun fire

from an old demolished church behind them! *BOOM!*
BOOM! BLAM! WHEEEEEEEEEEEEEEEEE, BOOM!!
Ratt-tat-tat-tah! Ratt-tat-tat-tah! WHEEEEEEEEEEE
BOOM! BOOM!

Then, it was quiet! Gray and white smoke filled the huge set. It was like walking in fog ~ Constance Ann had been separated from Elliot; and after quite a few minutes of searching they found one another. Next, they saw two human figures up on a balcony. When most of the smoke had cleared they saw their friend Mary Margaret gagged and bound to a pole ~ Andy stood a few feet away her, he held a toy paint pistol toward her armor plated chest! He yelled down to them!

"Finders keepers, I found her!" Elliot hurriedly aimed his bow and paint tip arrow at him! Andy shouted, "Do it! I'll hurt her! I will!" Elliot kept his arrow locked on Andy as Constance Ann yelled up to Andy,

"What do you want, Andrew?" Andy shook his head in disbelief. He spoke,

"What do you think? This is about . . . gum! I want another piece of bubble gum?"

"Gum?" shouted, Constance Ann! This is about me not giving you my bubble gum? Are you serious?"

"Do I look serious? Give me the gum or I will hurt

her!" Elliot shouted as he kept his arrow aimed at Andy, "We don't have any more gum! Mary Margaret gave you hers! Now you would hurt her? You're greedy, Andy! Come on, let her go!! You know, I can knock you off that balcony!"

"I'm not greedy!" shouted, Andy! "I'm spoiled! I get what I want! Constance Ann had no right to refuse me! My name is Andrew Welsh! I'm respected! Just who does she think she is refusing me?!! Now! Get me some gum! Nowwwww!" The little child rage was unstoppable, then *BUZZZ, PHOOF!* Fire exploded beneath Mary Margaret's feet! She wiggled to break free! Andy laughed uncontrollably! "Hah, hah, hah! You have only one arrow left, Elliot! What ya going to do . . . shoot me or shoot the water bag over her head!" Two little flaps opened to reveal a large plastic water bag! Then the flaps began to open and close unpredictable. Constance Ann nervously looked at Elliot who had now changed his aim toward the water bag! Constance Ann whispered to him, "Elliot, can you hit the water bag?"

"I don't know! Those door flaps keeps flapping. There's no rhythm!" He wiped his forehead with one of his forearms', he continued, "Well . . . so, what do I do? I can easy take him out!" Constance Ann lightly touched Elliot

arm and said,

"Hit, Mary Margaret!"

"What?!"

"Hit, Mary Margaret on her chest! That armor will protect her from any pain ~ trust me, Elliot!" Elliot slowly swung his aim toward Mary Margaret. It was obvious that he was confused! He hesitated! Constance Ann urged him on! "Do it! Do it, Elliot!" Then they saw Andy grab Mary Margaret by her cheeks! He squeezed them and shouted down to Elliot and Constance Ann!

"Poor, little Mary Margaret . . . huh, who will save you?" Then he aimed his paint gun at Elliot! He laughed and shouted, "Go ahead and shoot! Let your arrow fly! Ha-ha-ha-ha-ha!" The tension was beyond belief!

Constance Ann yelled at Elliot to shoot her best friend with his last arrow, but had offered no explanation to why! Andy Welsh was mentally lost with revenge and greed! Sweat mixed with dirt dripped from Elliot's face, nevertheless, through the confusion and all, he focused on his target and calmly asked,

"Constance Ann . . . you want a piece of gum?" Puzzled, Constance Ann slightly stammered over her words,

"Ah . . . yes . . . ah . . . of course, I do!" Elliot with his eyes focused on the target above, slowly turned his head toward Constance Ann. He spoke,

"Just, what I thought." Then, he unexpectedly socked her on the side of her face! Constance Ann's legs flew up in the air! Her head hit the ground and a wig fell off! Elliot walked over to the unconscious body and pulled a mask off the face! It was Andy! But dressed as Constance Ann in the clown outfit! Elliot then quickly turned and shot his last arrow up to the balcony! The arrow successfully passed through the opened flaps and burst the water bag! Gallons of water fell down onto Mary Margaret and drenched the fire below! And the water also short circuit something underneath Mary Margaret's armor chest plate and that short circuited the robot that was built in Andy's likeness! The robot slurred its last words,

"Noooooooooooooooooo." as it pointed his toy pistol toward the ground! Then!

"Hey, up there!" shouted, Elliot. "Are you alright?" The last of water fell over Mary Margaret's face and with it ~ it took Mary Margaret's face makeup off and Elliot saw what he already knew! Constance Ann and not Mary Margaret! She yelled down to him!

"How did you know? You had me concerned!" Suddenly, they heard,

"Connie! Elliot! Where were you guys? I've been hiding for hours! I even fell asleep! Hey, why are you tied up like that in my outfit? Hey! What did I miss? It was Mary Margaret! She had never been in danger ~ she walked toward Elliot, looked down at Andy in disbelief ~ Elliot spoke,

"Don't even ask." Then, he plopped down onto the ground with his legs crossed. He sighed with relief!

"Mary Margaret! Good to see ya, girl!" happily shouted a slopping wet Constance Ann!

Hours later after paramedics and fireman had taken Andy away; his father questioned the three kids from Johnsville, Vermont.

"You say all this was about gum?"

"Yes, sir," answered, Constance Ann as she dried her hair. She continued, "Bubble gum."

"But Andy is such a good kid. I give him anything he wants."

"Do you give him love?" asked Constance Ann. Mr. Welsh replied quickly,

"Of course, I do! He has everything! Look around! What do you see! He has this whole studio at his disposal!" Mr. Welsh was upset! He continued, "Well . . . go ahead, look around!" The three children looked around and Elliot spoke sadly,

"I don't see any kids." Then Mary Margaret spoke,

"Where there are kids, there's love."

"With kids," interrupted, Constance Ann, "you'll have many opportunities to give from the heart ~ to love as loving kids do.

"But," barked out, Mr. Welsh! Constance Ann interrupted again,

"And through interacting with other kids you can only grow in giving ~ and not some much in greed." Mr. Welsh threw his arms up ~

"Aaargh, love, greed bubble gum, they're all the same! Guards, escort these kids off my property at once!

Then Mr. Welsh turned to Elliot, he pointed his finger at him, "Young man, if I didn't know your father as well as I do, I would tell him of this incident. But, I won't!" After that, he stormed off! Mary Margaret spoke,

"Wow, all this was over gum?"

"No," answered, Constance Ann. "Gum was just used as the issue. I hurt his feelings when I didn't give him my gum. He saw it as a sign of rejection. The kind rejection of not being cared about or even loved."

"But, you didn't mean it like that, Connie."

"I know, I didn't, Mary Margaret. But he didn't ~ he need love and not toys or bubble gum ~ love, my dearest friend." Constance Ann took a deep breath and asked, "Elliot, how . . ."

"How did I know that Andy was dressed in disguised and it wasn't really you just before I hit him? To be frank, I didn't. But, do you remember when we fell into the water? Well, Andy fell in too and all of our paint was washed off!" Constance Ann interrupted, "And when you saw the paint on his shirt you knew that couldn't have been him?" Elliot interrupted her, "There never were any teenagers, only him, he staged it all! And we were separated long enough for him to kidnap you and make the switch. I then noticed that there was paint all over the clown costume. Then, I began to wonder, but the final straw was when he accepted my gum offer. You would never have been concern about anything except for the safety of a friend. So I belted him one!"

"You're too, cool," excitedly shouted Mary Margaret! "You're just too cool!" Elliot plucked the string to his bow with happiness ~ then he raised his eyebrows casually!

After the security guards had allowed them to change back into their own clothes, they waited for Lincoln (Mary Margaret's older brother, 18 years old) to drive up in the rental car! *HONK! HONK!*

"Lincoln . . . alright!" shouted Elliot!

"Get in gang!" cried, Lincoln. He continued, "How did your day go? Did you have fun? Oh, here's some gum for you guys!" Elliot looked at the gum and slowly smiled,

"Ahh, naw." He shook his head.

"What about you girls," asked, Lincoln. Constance Ann shook her as she tried to smile ~ "Mmmmm, naw." Mary Margaret reached for a piece of gum. She noticed Elliot and Constance Ann, they stared at her. She stopped; then, asked,

"Lincoln, do you love me?" Lincoln smiled brightly,

"Of course, I do, Mary Margaret. Why?"

"Good . . . I'll just take that piece of gum then!"

Lincoln spoke, "I love you all of you, guys!" Then Constance Ann and Elliot both reached out their hands for a piece of gum. They all giggled as they chewed their gum surrounded by one another with the spirit of love!

EPILOGUE:

As Hollywood goes, love goes. People chew gum, people don't chew gum ~ Greed lives, greed dies, and love has nothing better to do, except but to love ~

*And that's a take!

The end! *(Hollywood term meaning – print it)*

Follow our three geniuses, Constance Ann, Mary Margaret and Elliot into their next adventure ~
'Constance Ann in School'

Introducing . . .

CONSTANCE ANN ©

BONUS STORY

THE FURTHER ADVENTURES OF CONSTANCE ANN

Illustrated
and written
by edwin gilven

CONSTANCE ANN OUT WEST ©

Illustrated
and written
by edwin gilven

CONSTANCE ANN IN SEATTLE ©

Illustrated
and written
by edwin gilven